1

A Novella

Jessica Bonder

Broke Witch

Copyright © 2022 Jessica Bonder

All rights reserved.

ISBN-13: 979-8-9861105-3-0

Cover design by Savannalore

Printed in the U.S.A.

For more titles and inquiries, please visit:

www.thirtywestph.com

"It is to be said that witches are not generally rich for this reason: that the devils like to show their contempt for the Creator by buying witches for the lowest possible price."

—from *The Malleus Maleficarum of Heinrich Kramer and James Sprenger*, Part I, Question 18

eave it to a wild little girl in a bright pink snowsuit. Tongue hanging out. Panting. Yelling for me to wait. Scrambling up the snowbank, Rose lets out a roar.

"Watch," I say. "Snow's dirty."

On all fours, transformed into a dinosaur, Rose has something to say. Yes, witch, she's well aware.

"What do I look like—a kid?"

Witch and girl, tall and short, two return to the complex. Rose tells me *Indomitus Rexes* have scales the color of snow. "That's why they love the winter. No predators can spot them!" Rose indicates a square of sidewalk outside her unit. "Wait right here! I'll go inside and get Crystal!"

There, I wait for Rose. There, was a flash of memory: Rose's mother on their porch before she disappeared. Right there, she was sobbing—sobbing into her phone—a figure across the complex whose name I didn't know. Unloading bags from my trunk, I overheard her mother's terror: "I'm really scared. I don't have anybody."

For reasons I can't explain, I ignored my magic. Should have gone to help her mother, invoked a healing spell, three generations confined to a unit, and clearly something wrong, but instead, I went inside to put away groceries. Overheard her terror and chose to walk away. Walk away. Ignore.

Terror is none of my business.

Our units in the complex are identical to each other. One story. Squat. Gray. Shingles peeling off roofs. Porches painted white. Satellite dishes. Chairs. Equidistant, they face each other in a giant square—four units to a building, four buildings in total—sixteen units squared about the parking lot. A gazebo in the middle is like a pupil in a black eye. Wires overhead from which sneakers hung. Whose feet did they belong?

They'd been there forever.

And here comes Rose on the very same porch emerging with her Crystal, breaking the conjured image of her mother, crying. As if it were a dream. As if it hadn't happened. Crystal is a big plastic dinosaur cradled in Rose's arms, an example of *Indomitus Rex* earlier described.

"Crystal can't go in the snow because of her computer chip." She turns her over to show me. "If you scan this chip with your phone, you can get cool dinosaur facts. Dr. Wu at Jurassic Park Lab gives you all the latest."

I saw the first Jurassic Park movie when I was in middle school. Read the Michael Crichton book. Taught myself the John Williams score on the piano. I was a weird, obsessive kid who had to learn everything. The boys mocked me on the bus. I struggled to make friends. A curse into adulthood I simply could not break.

Rose decides to bring Crystal back inside. "Even the moisture in the air could mess up her chip." Again, she directs me to wait in front of her unit. I hear her grandmother's voice behind a television. I can't tell what she's saying. The TV drowns her out. Rose reemerges on her porch spanking empty gloves. "That's that, put it away. Won't be getting ruined."

"Anyway, I should get going," I say. "It's really cold out here. Should have worn a heavier coat. Or a nice snowsuit like yours."

Turn on my heels. Feel for my keys. Time to go inside. Traverse the lot chemically treated to keep us from slipping. Soon after we got letters advising bottled water. Toxic runoff from the melt had seeped into our tap.

Rose sprints ahead of me to my parking space. Every unit was granted one space. One car is permitted per family. Fine for a family of one but what of a family of three? Or what of a family of two since the disappearance? Rose stops at my Hyundai Accent. Navy blue. Dented. A beater.

"Why is your car still covered?"

Figured the sun would melt the snow whenever it came out. But day after day, the firmament hung like a weighted blanket. Flannel dense. Heavy. Remember when the skies were blue? About how dark this winter was, everyone was talking. Dogs howled at the sun mistaking it for the moon. Cats screeched at raccoons digging around garbage.

"How about we clean your car off together?" Rose pushes hair from her face. Her knit hat is an ice cream cone. Red pom-pom, the cherry. Her eyes are brown like mine, but I never looked like Rose. Always scrawny, and skinny, I shot up like a weed and maintained a reedy look into my adulthood. While Rose was stocky. Cheeks rosy as her name. "I'll go get Nonna's scraper. You get yours, okay?"

Thumb snow off the keyhole and open up my trunk. An avalanche of week-old snow as the dark mouth widens. And there it was, the box. If I brought it into my unit, I'd have to accept Ma's death. I wasn't ready, no. I was still in mourning.

"What's that box?" Rose again at my side, Nonna's scraper propped on her shoulder like a baseball bat.

"Those are my mother's things. She passed away."

"Oh."

Get my scraper. Short, stubby, cracked, in desperate need of replacement. Close my trunk with a slam. "Let's get to work!" Rose rallies.

Rose is a good kid. That or she's very lonely. How she languished in front of her unit when I said I was leaving. Raced ahead to my car. Offered to help me clean. Lonely I was as Rose and wanting a companion. And here she was, Rose.

The daughter I never had.

I slide big chunks of snow across the roof of my beater. Rose whacks the chunks as they fall to the ground.

"What grade are you?"

"Third."

Swipe. Slide. Whack.

"That makes you—"

"Eight. Turning nine in June."

An urge then to ask Rose what happened to her mother. But how do you ask a question when you fear the answer? The answer cannot be good. I knew how these things went. A pattern was observed at the complex.

Things went and nothing stopped them.

Curses. Secrets. Mysteries. Hide the ugly truth. Can't have any poor people in a rich people town. Stuck the complex across from the quarry where no one would see us. Behind the quarry was a firing range where police practiced on targets. Targets are shaped like people. Bullseyes over hearts. Most days it was hard to tell if it was bullets or rocks. I learned to cover my ears. I learned how to play dead. I learned to get by in a place I didn't want to live but lived and lived and lived.

What choice did a broke witch have?

I got my unit by chance. Out of the blue, a phone call from the New Jersey Fair Housing Division. An agent down in Trenton said she had a unit available. "Are you familiar with Baronsville?" Before she could show me the unit, I said I would take it. No questions asked. I needed a place to live. And who but Rose the very first one to say hello to me? In kindergarten then, she waved.

We take a break on the curb. Rose picks icicles off my fender. Offers me one as a lollipop. "Here, you take the bigger one. After all, we're friends." Rose licks her icicle and says it tastes like cherry. No, watermelon.

"Ow, my baby tooth." Rose gives her tooth a waggle. "Did you know it's fake? Tooth Fairy isn't real. Neither is Santa Claus, but I knew that already."

Rose leaps up. Dusts snow off her legs like sand at the beach. "Hey, look at those icicles up there! Those are big as swords!"

"True. But how would we reach the roof?"

"What if we got a ladder?"

"I'm not getting a ladder, Rose."

Rose makes a frowny face.

"Why not? You're an adult."

"What about the ones hanging from my railing?"

We head to my porch. With a wooden ramp installed, my entire unit is modified to meet ADA standards. The toilet seat's a contraption for someone in a wheelchair. My shower has handlebars like a stationary bicycle. The tub has swinging doors like a Western saloon.

Rose snaps two large icicles off my railing. We lance them in the air, jousting to save the kingdom. "The kingdom of what?" "The complex!" Wasn't it obvious? Even more obvious was the fact I'd neglected to wear gloves. Blood drained from my fingertips, blanching them white as turnips.

Her grandmother appears at a distance beckoning for Rose. From here, she is a shadow in a doorframe. "I need you, Rose! Please come home now, Rose!" Rose transforms into a bear cub recalled to her den. Drops her icicle sword as she takes off my porch, shattering it into pieces that skid across the lot. "Bye, Fern!" she yells as she runs, waving her glove in the air.

My name rang as a bell resounds across the complex. An explosion from the quarry ends the echo in a blast. The beeping of a truck driving in reverse. There to pick up rocks.

Or was it target practice?

I have three new messages.

First message: *Good morning, I'm calling from the Department of Labor regarding your unemployment claim. Did you quit your job or were you laid off? This directly affects your benefits. Please call us at extension two-two-six as soon as you get this message.*

Second message: *Hello, this message is from the health clinic. It looks like your Medicaid coverage isn't updated in our system. Please call us to confirm your insurance.*

Third message*: Your food stamps are due to expire at the end of the month. Please call the Office of Social Services to verify your status. Remember to have your case number ready.*

Saved messages: eleven.

Waiting to pay at Rite Aid.

On the counter is a bucket of individually wrapped roses for Valentine's Day. A handwritten sign is taped to the bucket: WOODEN ROSES $1.00. The realistic petals are delicate slivers of wood, painted pink and red. Why do they stay perfect? The roses were dead trees. The woman in front of me is purchasing six for herself. "I think these will look nice in a vase. What do you think?"

Mum's the checkout person. Her job is to ring things up, not advise on home decor. The checkout person, I realize, lives with me at the complex. Mum's an older lady I've seen at the mailboxes. I could point out her car, a tan Honda Civic, could say between these lines is where it's meant to park.

"How come they're coming up $1.18? The bucket says a dollar." The woman turns the bucket. "See? Says a dollar." Mum doesn't know why the computer is saying $1.18. They stare at the digital display screen together. Are you seeing what I'm seeing? Even with Jersey sales tax, the price cannot be right.

Suddenly, a secret door opens. The store manager appears. In a move befitting a psychic, she opens another register. Price discrepancy? Sure. "I'll take you over here, ma'am."

The tension drops like a curtain at a play's conclusion.

My turn. I step up to the plate. Dump my drugs on the counter. Caffeine pills, antacids, sleep aids, ibuprofen, store-brand Pepto-Bismol, saliva-inducing mouth rinse. These are on top of the drugs I picked up in the back. Duloxetine. Amlodipine. Enalapril. Levothyroxine. Each is in its white paper bag with a printed prescription stapled on top.

Being alive is expensive if you can't do it naturally.

Mum starts scanning my pile like she's seen it all before. Does she know who I am? In any event, I'd like to know more about my neighbor. Starting with Mum's name. As it turns out, it's Reba. I read it off her vest paired with a hello.

"Hello, Reba."

No response. Scans.

"Hi, Reba. I live with you at the complex."

"Reba's not my name. I'm just borrowing the vest."

"Oh. Well. My name is Fern."

"Cash, credit, or check?"

"The unit nearest the dumpster."

"Whenever you're ready."

I pay in cash. It takes a long time for Not-Reba to count it. It had been a minute since someone paid with literal money. The Rite Aid in which we stood was on the rich side of town, far away from the quarry and the firing range. On this side of Baronsville, shoppers had their choice of plastic.

Not-Reba hands me my change. Why won't she tell me her name? I can only think of one reason, the reason it always is. Same witch, different day.

"Is it because I'm a witch?"

Witch hangs in the air like a sneaker on a wire. Not-Reba says they're out of bags and shoves across my items. When I see plastic bags beside her register. Could grab the whole lot in my fist.

"Next customer in line!"

The man who comes up behind me is buying a single light bulb. Make way. My manly body needs room. Unfolding his fat wallet, he looks me up and down. This is what a witch looks like, thinks the entitled man. But where's the pointy hat?

Two black vultures are on the roof against the gray expanse. Black vultures have been out in droves all winter. Stalking Quarry Street like dinosaurs in packs. Nineteen is the record count in the complex parking lot. I do not know who held the record, it's hearsay.

For fun, we don't count cars. We count birds of prey.

Mr. C avoids me until his car breaks down. Then the old man has no choice but to ask the witch for help. I lived in the unit next to his. Could I buy his groceries? He stands on my porch and clasps his hands in bony supplication.

"Help me, witch! I don't want to die of starvation!" I tell him I'll think about it. I don't want to die either. Have you seen how people drive around here? Plus, it costs me gas. Another thing is, I see how you blank me. Duck into your unit when you see me out walking. But now you need something from me—a little unfair, don't you think? For you to expect me to do it?

"Give me a day. I'll get back to you."

That night I hear his wails of hunger through the wall we shared. What would he do if I said no? Or what if I said yes? Beholden to the witch, he'd be, for the rest of his life—or as long as the bony old man needed groceries from ShopRite.

The next day, I appear on his porch in my long black coat. Mr. C grabs at his chest when he opens the door, a fistful of a plaid sweater.

Mr. C relaxes. Tense one, Mr. C.

"I'll do it but not for free. There's a

surcharge of ten bucks."

"Ten dollars!" Mr. C recoils. "But you're my neighbor!"

"Ten bucks, final offer. This is work for me."

Mr. C hesitates as if he has a choice. But what choice does he have? I was the youngest person that had a car at the complex. Most neighbors are elderly or on disability.

"What you're doing is immoral. You're taking advantage of neighbors."

"Taking advantage? How? It's you who needs my help."

"Asking for money is evil. Money is the devil's work."

Ah yes, the stereotype. Witches were possessed by Satan. Where'd you hear that, Medieval Times? Raising your chicken drumstick?

"Okay, no problem. Guess you're not interested."

Abruptly turn. Retreat. Close the door to my unit. Crash on my couch. Nap. Awake an hour later to a sound on my screen door. An envelope with cash and a grocery list slides down to my feet. Well, well, well. What do you know? Cavorting with the devil. Seems someone needs to eat.

I purchase his groceries at ShopRite. Bananas, oats, low-sodium potato chips, instant coffee, two-percent milk, and a loaf of bread. What about something for dinner? I guess he didn't eat dinner. An insectoid quality to him. Hunch of a praying mantis. Flightiness of a moth.

I deliver Mr. C's groceries and skim myself a sandwich. Slather on peanut butter and arrange banana rounds. An Elvis Presley Special. Why not? He'd never notice.

I think about his son.

Mr. C has a son who lives on the rich side of Baronsville. Although he has the means, he doesn't help his father. Mr. C told me why in one of his less-scared moments.

"My son doesn't want to be jumped. That's why he doesn't come round."

This golden son's assumption was someone else would do it—would help his elderly father if he should need the help. And here I was, helping. Chew. Swallow. Chew. Which is why I don't feel evil asking for ten dollars. Elvis was delicious.

▼

I open my kitchen window and apologize to Rose. Rose had been banging my railing. Since the day of the car cleaning, Rose would summon me: ring my bell, knock on my door, stomp the boards of my porch, roll rocks up my ramp. Ring again, pound again, never, never give up. My boards developed creaks. My dirt ran out of rocks. Rose knocked over my shovel like my cat did books.

Rose peers in on tippy toes. "You have a nice kitchen!"

"Really? It's a pigsty."

"Pigs are clean. They're also very smart."

Rose and her animal facts. Spoken like a true third grader.

A meow.

"Is that your cat?"

Chance jumps on the counter. Saunters over to the window and presses his nose to the screen. Eyes grass green and gleaming. Fur black as night, unless the sun morphed him into mahogany. Preferred the kitchen counter. At all times, Chance knew where you were.

"Why does he only have one ear?"

"Someone didn't take care of him. The shelter said he had an ear infection that went untreated. The ear collapsed on itself and shriveled up to nothing."

"That's sad."

"It is. But he can hear just fine."

"White cats with blue eyes are deaf. Had one when I was little. It got hit by a car."

She's so young. What a morbid little girl.

"Boo!"

Chance jumps off the counter.

"Scaredy cat! Scaredy cat! Scaredy cat!" Rose tips back her head and emits a devilish laugh.

Then a pair of flapping dragons comes into my view. "This is Frank and Francine. Want to come out so you can meet them?"

Kid fingers work the wings, green fabric, and bedazzled. Forked tongues sewn of felt, orange as parking cones. Plastic button eyes. Stuffed tails.

"I'll give you to the count of a hundred. One...two...three..."

Rose counts on my porch as I bundle up. From anywhere in my unit, you can hear anything. It's small. Ten strides front to back—twelve strides if you're short—but my legs were trees. I walked around on pines.

A couch purchased secondhand sits in the living room. Towers of used books. A small coffee table I'd found on the curb someone had put out. Leaning in the corner, my witch's broom, long dormant. My altar, filmed beneath the dust. A floor lamp.

A sunken mattress on a metal frame occupies the bedroom. A closet into which clothes are shoved. A mirror shrouded in mourning. A light bulb with a string.

A folding table and chair are in the galley kitchen. One placemat on the table. One cup, one plate, one fork. Sticky linoleum floor. A smell coming from the drain. A stove that will not light without the strike of a match. A leaky refrigerator required manual defrosting.

Rose and I trudge through the snow behind her unit, Frank, and Francine soaring on her hands. Turns out they are married and expecting a baby. They're naming the baby Diamond.

Rose runs backward as her dragons get caught up in the wind. Frank, tossed sideways, breaks his back on a tree. To heal him, Rose fashions an icicle splint and sprinkles him with snow. Before this, Rose informs me that Frank got sick from rat poison.

"Pretend rat poison?"

"Real rat poison. Come look."

Rose shows me the rat poison box nestled against the foundation. She reads its contents aloud, written in tiny print. All our units had these black boxes. All this time I lived at the complex, I assumed they were utilities from the electric company. Often I marveled how a housing complex as neglected and unkempt and garbage prone as ours didn't have a rat problem. Now I understood. Rat poison was out in the open this entire time.

We sit on a patch of shoveled sidewalk. Frank is doing better but Frank is not okay. Rose tells me Frank's history. Frank is shy, for starters. He'd been bullied as a kid dragon. As the runt of the litter had to fight his siblings for food.

"He can't stop thinking about what happened years ago!" Rose clutches Frank's wings to his head as if in agony. "He can't get it out of his head! He's the weakest dragon!"

I tell Frank he has to do a mega blast. A mega blast, I'd just learned from Rose, is when a dragon gathers all their strength and expels a powerful blast of fire. A blast so strong, so powerful, you have to take cover on the sidewalk. You have to believe in yourself. We know you can do it, Frank.

On the first attempt, Frank fails. He doesn't have it in him.

On the second attempt, Frank succeeds. His blast shakes every tree.

To make sure Frank is okay after his mega blast, I listen to his heart with a pretend stethoscope. "If you can hear Frank's heart," Rose says, "that means he's not a ghost."

I say I can hear his heart.

"Good, he's not a ghost!"

Growing up, my sister and I had a stethoscope. A real one, like it, came from a doctor's office. We'd sit on a log like turtles and listen to each other's hearts. Of all the things I saved, I saved the stethoscope.

Sometimes I'll check my heart. Am I yet a ghost?

Here are the questions I am asked to get food stamps:

Are you a US Citizen? Are you a veteran? Are you pregnant or planning to become pregnant? Are you paying child support? Have you voluntarily quit a job within the last sixty days? Have you given away or sold a family heirloom in the last six months? How long have you lived at your current residence? Do you own a car? Do you receive Social Security payments? Do you own any properties other than your main residence? Have you received gifts of money from family members? Do you have a savings or checking account? Approximately how much money is currently in that account? Are you paid biweekly or monthly? When was your last date of pay? Approximately how much money were you paid, pre-tax? When was your last pay date prior to that? Was the amount you earned approximately the same? How much is your mortgage? Does that include taxes? How much are your taxes per year? Do you purchase homeowner's insurance? Approximately how much is your homeowner's insurance? Do you pay for your own gas, electricity, and water? How much do you pay for gas? How much do you pay for electricity? How much do you pay for water? Does anyone live at your residence besides you? Has anyone lived with you or moved out in the last six months? Are you supporting anyone?

The Social Services Office is on the same block as the county courthouse. When I arrive at the office, my existence is acknowledged through a Plexiglas window. Dried spit and snot are splattered. Beneath this window, a latex-gloved hand slips me an old brown clipboard. A Xeroxed form is attached. I fill out the form and return it. They buzz me into the waiting room.

The waiting room is packed on a Tuesday afternoon. A snoozing man like I've seen on the train is tucked into himself. A teenage girl rocks a baby in a stroller. Her boyfriend manspreads into an otherwise open seat. A grandmother stares off into space hugging her purse to her chest. Her grandson swings his legs chattering away in Spanish. Something about *escuela*. An older woman in a yellow sari is accompanied by her husband. He wears an eye patch, a hefty wad of gauze crisscrossed with medical tape. They do not speak to each other. Happily, married couple.

I manage to find a seat.

Molded plastic chairs are bolted to the floor. The floor is filthy linoleum. You can see the cement underneath where feet have trod the most. One small window high up near the ceiling is sealed shut and fitted with bars. The air I breathe is the breath of other lungs packed into a very small space. Smells of body odor. Smells of a dirty diaper. No TV to watch. No magazines to read. Instead, a broken clock in the middle of the wall tricks you into hope. They're running ahead of time! Just kidding, the clock is wrong.

My name is shouted. My name is shouted twice. I stand at the same time as the other Fern. What are the odds two Ferns would be getting food stamps on the same day? To clarify, they read surnames. My doppelgänger sits. Here they have very little patience. Do not push their limits. Hurry, squeeze by, excuse me, pardon, sorry, could you move your stroller, thanks.

I walk down a dark hall toward a lady at a desk. It is pushed against the wall. She takes my driver's license. Checks my name off a list. Doesn't look at me as she does this. Returns my ID by holding it out. Here, take this thing, I don't want it. Points a single finger to direct me where to go. A room at the end of the hall is just like a waiting room. Bodies packed wall to wall, it's called the training room. Once again, I sit.

Now it is time to learn.

As if by magic, a video starts playing. A woman in a pantsuit demonstrates how to use her SNAP card at the grocery store. How to swipe it at check-out and punch in your PIN. The woman in the video warns you: never share your PIN.

After the video, we line up at the door. One by one, we're issued our SNAP cards. The lady from the hall holds out a keypad to enter a PIN of our choosing. Never share it, she reminds us. Recert's in six months. As if we're not worth the effort of four more syllables.

Recertification, say it. We deserve the non-abbreviated version for putting up with this hell.

I spot the woman with the one-eyed dog. She's out walking her Cyclops. Little white fluffy thing. A single, shiny black eye. Socket for the second eye overgrown with fur, like an unmarked grave in a field. Grassy to no one's notice.

"Oh, hello!" She seeks my face for a name. I catch the dimming in her eyes when she's given up. One side of her face is drooping. Did she have a stroke? I remember her in a wheelchair pushed around by Peter, Cyclops tied to the armrest like a boat in tow, going around the complex in their parade.

"Aren't we glad we got out today?" Her wide hips shift from side to side beneath her winter coat. She's wearing fuzzy slippers, heels smashed-down and dirty. No more do they look like slippers. More paws. How fur grows on rotten fruit after a good while. How anything can be anything if you give it time.

As for her husband, Peter rescues worms in the rain. One day I looked outside. The rain was coming down hard. There was Peter in the parking lot looking around for something. Had Peter dropped his glasses? His wallet? I popped my umbrella and ventured out, squinting through the showers. "You okay

Peter? Need help?" Peter looked up, smiling. "I'm saving worms from drowning. Just something I like to do. All creatures great and small."

He resumed his worm rescue.

Peter is an old hippie. He fixes bicycles for a living. I imagine he met his wife at a place like Woodstock. Did tons of drugs and wound up here, broke at the end of their lives. Peter wears John Lennon glasses. Speaks softly and treads lightly. If he wasn't such a hippie, I'd say he was a wizard.

The men in the complex are losing their minds.

"Who did a big yawn? Who did a big yawn?"

"Who wants to play? Who wants to play?"

"Trainer, where are you boy? Where's my good boy Trainer?"

This madness goes on all day; my spell seems to be working; that's what the men get for not curbing their dogs where little kids are playing.

For I had had enough of having to warn Rose. Look here Rose and be careful Rose and watch the snowbank is dirty. I do not take spells lightly. I know the depths of my powers. What I can say is this: the snowbank is now clean.

And what about the men? Doomed to talk to mutts. At their beck and call, cleaning up their mess. A smile spreads on my face.

Yes, my spell is working.

By another spell, I find a dentist who accepts Medicaid.

I expect hers to be a junky operation. Pulling teeth in the back of a van. Instead, she's in an upscale medical building in the rich part of Baronsville. One of those buildings has windows that mirror your reflection. A self-conscious making building as if it's sizing you up. Are you worthy of entering me? Do you know what building I am?

It occurs to me that I would have been more comfortable in the back of a van. Being in super clean places puts me on edge. For I was not super clean. Showered once a week. Dressed in all black because black absorbed the colors of whatever stains were on me. Taking a course in color theory wasn't a total loss. For a time, I considered going to art school. Had my portfolio ready and then the guilt kicked in. I came from a working-class family, a single mother at that. What right did I have to think that I could be an artist?

In this reverie, I walk into myself. Boom. Straight into a mirrored door. Check my startled reflection to see if I broke my nose. Still hooked? We're good. If not a little sore.

The Medical Arts lobby is lush with exotic

plants like a resort in Bali. Not that I'd been to Bali but that's how I imagined it. More body-checking mirrors lining the walls. Two steel elevators. A directory between them. Names and office numbers, lit.

Perfect Smiles: 3A.

Alone in the elevator, then walking down the hall. Could hear a pin drop in this place. Is anybody here? Perfect Smiles. Check-in and wait to be called. Pick a chair in the corner.

My life was comprised of waiting.

While listening for my name, a gentleman makes an entrance. How he looks spells money. Boomer age. Tailored shirt. Navy blue blazer. Narrow slacks. Suede loafers. "Love your hair and nails." He checks himself in with Audra, the receptionist. Audra has hair extensions and long fake nails with rhinestones. I highly doubt Mr. Executive thinks she looks attractive.

Before sitting down, Mr. Executive brushes off his chair. Not with his hand, he does it with a brush. Like the kind of old-fashioned barbers. Sits. Pockets his brush. Looks me up and down. Then he looks away.

My name is called from the back.

The dentist asks do I floss, and I answer

no. I'm not going to lie. My mouth is full of blood. She measures my gum pockets with a pointy tool. "You're at a five. You'll never get back to a two." The higher the number, she explains, the worse my gum recession. "If you don't start to floss, you're going to have tooth loss."

It's then I want to say: I suffer from depression. The fact that I am here is a big achievement. A life ahead of dentures, can we discuss my feelings?

But a dentist isn't a therapist. Someone with an emotional life couldn't work in this place. Refrigerator cold. Framed photographs of grayscale mountains. A gigantic free-standing vase. On a flat-screen television, snobby people taste food. Three gods behind a table send down their judgments. What has been picked to watch during your appointment.

"I have to go do an exam. Then I'll come back, and we can finish your cleaning." The dentist, I should mention, was cleaning my teeth herself, as her hygienist had quit, and she couldn't find a replacement. I wondered if it had anything to do with her accepting Medicaid patients. Like our teeth were so godawful the hygienist couldn't take it anymore.

There I am, sitting in the chair, waiting for the dentist to return, and I hear the entire conversation ensuing with Mr. Executive. His room is one room over. The rooms here have no doors. "For now, I'm doing consulting. I much prefer the freedom." The dentist chimes in. "I completely understand. My husband says the same thing." They're doing so much talking, she can't be checking his teeth. If she were checking his teeth, I wouldn't be hearing this.

Five, ten, fifteen minutes pass. I stand up and stretch. Consider walking over and reminding her I exist. *Sure took a long time*, I want to say when she breezes in. Instead, I sit in the chair and have her lecture me. I need to do a better job of taking care of my teeth. Four months, she recommends. I want to see you in four months.

"Four months," she tells Audra at the desk, wishing me the best of luck. But I'm coming back, aren't I? Why are you wishing me luck? On the counter is a rock formation that holds the dentist's business cards. I touch the rocks. Fake. Resin reproductions. Trompe l'oeil of balanced chakras.

Audra asks how it went today.

"I'm embarrassed about not flossing my teeth. Why is it so hard for me to get my act together?"

"Fern, let me tell you something. My whole life doctors have been telling me to lose weight. Do I lose weight? I don't. I've never looked good as you."

"It's kind of you to say that."

What I don't tell Audra is I was thin because I didn't eat. Food tasted bland to me. Eating was a chore.

"It's nice talking to an actual person. At home, it's just me and my cat. It's strange not talking to anyone for days on end."

Audra frowns with her eyes. "You can talk with me anytime."

But how would I talk to Audra? Call her on the phone. She's the dental receptionist. Wouldn't that be weird?

When my mother was alive, we went to the same park. We knew every tree, every bend in the trail, every stone underfoot.

We knew when something was wrong.

That day a dark spirit hung over the forest. A young man had committed suicide by hanging. The young man was Black. The town was on pins and needles thinking of the very worst. His father released a statement. His son had always been troubled and had battled drug addiction since middle school. Despite how it appears, it isn't what you think.

Imagine a sigh of relief. Oh good, he took his own life. Not as bad as we thought. We can go back to our lives.

I met my mother at the park. The first thing I said when I saw her was: "Did you hear about the young man?" She said she knew the young man's father. Small world. "You never know who you're speaking to." She offered me an unfinished granola bar. "Want it? It's good." Anything that my mother offered, I would always accept.

"It's okay." She took my hand. "We'll offer an intention."

On my way to the park, I had to fight back tears. I wondered if I should bring up my declining mental health. How lonely I was. How lost. Then thought, Don't go there, Fern. You already brought up the young man. Wasn't that enough?

"Wasn't there a stand of trees here?"

"Ash trees," said Ma. "Diseased. They had to cut them down."

The air was redolent of the former ashes. Cut stumps along the ground sat in beds of sawdust. Downed trees like mortal losses I couldn't comprehend.

We came upon slabs of white quartz. Big, beautiful slabs, milky with gray veins. Glaciers millions of years ago deposited them here. "Let's ground ourselves," said Ma. We got on our hands and knees and pressed our foreheads to the quartz. Once grounded, we rose to cast a circle. Sent our cone of energy to the young man who had died. When we drew up the circle, a light came through the trees. It dappled our stone-pocked faces.

We continued on the trail.

I asked my mother if she remembered the time we went hiking in the Delaware Water Gap.

"Not that I recall."

"Really?"

We climbed roots as if they were stairs.

I couldn't believe my mother didn't remember the incident. It was a story we told for years.

"We thought the trail was shorter than it turned out to be. The sun went down, and we were stuck. We had to yell for help. You don't remember this?"

Again, Ma shook her head.

A shadow passed overhead as I had the thought: was my mother losing her memory? Was this how it starts?

We came to the bank of a lake. A man squatting at its edge swatted at fish with a net.

"People do things. They do things with others or alone. But they get out and do things."

My mother was right. How come I hadn't thought to squat by a lake and swat at fish with a net? Yet all I could think was that's weird. What is that guy going to do with a bucket of fish?

We crossed a wooden bridge. Our four feet thumped together. Stopped to peer over the edge. See anything? See fish? A waterfall where the lake fed into the river. White water rushing, tumbling. Moss grew on the rocks.

"I'm thinking of getting a jet ski."

"Really, Ma? A jet ski?"

"I think it'd be fun. Riding it on the water. Maybe I can ride it here. I'll have to check the rules."

Continued around the lake. A heron, angled legs. Waterfowl. Life. Clouds. Sun. Sky.

We noticed the same man loading his bucket into his SUV. The rear bumper was peppered with self-made advertisements for his pet sitting service. What kind of pet eats live fish? A Komodo dragon?

Ma said her latest thing was watching YouTube videos. Her favorite series was called *Learn Your Land*. It's a naturalist telling you all about the different properties of things that grow from the ground.

"Luke just cut his hair. He has one of those hole earrings." I asked her how old she thought Luke was. "Late twenties, I would say. He's very enthusiastic."

What had I been doing? I could have been a naturalist.

"Haven't seen any mushrooms today." Ma poked around with a stick. Only stiff cadavers from last season. No new, no fresh.

Ma told the story of how she'd found a

giant puffball. Large as a volleyball. Completely edible. "I have a picture of it on my phone. Let me see if I can find it." She stopped to swipe. "Whoops. Guess I took a video. Anyway, here it is."

In the video, my mother stands still as a Grecian statue. She presents the giant puffball like a sacred artifact. "A giant puffball," she says. And that is all she says.

Oh Ma, it's a video. You're allowed to move.

My sister's husband, Mark, boxed up Ma's things. 'Odds-and-ends' he'd found inside her house.

"Items had no value beyond the personal."

Mark worked in finance, and this is how he spoke: like everything in life should be appraised for value. Including people.

Mark was the one responsible for getting my mother into a nursing home. What it took was cold hard cash pressed into administrative palms. The sale of her house went to the place where Ma would eventually die. It took her every last cent to do what she would have done anyway.

As for my mother's jet ski, Mark kept it for himself. Did he want the jet ski? Fine. He could have the jet ski. My grief was just too great.

I had no will to fight.

Nevertheless, the box of 'odds-and-ends' they asked me to pick up. Swing by on a weekend. We'll leave the garage door open.

I parked my beater on Locust Court and entered their garage. A cardboard box labeled 'MA'S THINGS' beside our mother's jet ski. Neon green with a big black seat hitched up to a trailer. How could I resist the chance? Its aura drew me in.

I straddled the seat, gripping the handlebars, leaning to one side, then to the other, and envisioned running a course. At a table on the shoreline, judges give me tens. Ten! Ten! Ten! A medal around my neck. Biting to check for gold. Chocolate filling my mouth...

"What are you doing?"

"I wasn't—"

"No, it's okay. Didn't mean to scare you."

It's Mark. Buff in a white T-shirt, basketball shorts, Adidas slider sandals, standing in the doorway like a Roman emperor.

He motioned to the jet ski with his coffee mug. "Ever rode one before?"

"I'm actually scared of water."

"Why be scared? With the WaveRunner, you're riding along on the surface!"

Mark mimicked the weaving motion I was doing a moment before. A tingling in my ears. The heat coming up my neck. How long was he standing there watching me play pretend?

Yanking down my coat, I dismounted the jet ski. Turned away my backside to strategically lift the box. Mark looked out the garage.

"Up, look who it is."

Pulling into the driveway was Mabel in her black Chevy Tahoe. Mabel hit the brakes as I walked directly toward her, giving her no choice but to roll down her window.

"Oh, hello," said Mabel. "See you've got the box."

She propped her big sunglasses on the crown of her head. Her nose, smooth as a slide, used to be hooked like mine. Her lips looked extra plump. Her skin was taut as a drum. She was wearing a puffer coat with an embroidered patch on the sleeve. The silhouette of a mountain. And diamond stud earrings winked like eyes with her every movement.

Her engine ticked, hummed. We stared at each other blankly.

"Ma's WaveRunner," I said. "It's actually pretty nice."

"Mark's going to sell it. Do some research on the current market value. Don't need another toy."

"Oh."

"Fern, listen, I'd love to chat but I'm sort of in a hurry."

Besides my sister in the front seat, a

bulging shopping bag. She'd been to the mall, her temple. She turned away from me and rifled for a purchase. Digging, digging, digging. How deep was that bag? Probably bottomless.

"But Mabel, it's Saturday. Don't you have a second?"

Finding whatever it was, she turned back to me. A thing for her phone. "Fine, Fern. What is it?"

"I'd like to visit sometime."

"The baby," she snapped. "You couldn't handle it."

"Handle what?"

"The screaming, the diaper changes. The visit would not be pleasant. Believe me, it's not a good idea for you to be coming over."

At that very moment, the baby was sleeping peacefully. Cushioned in his designer car seat like a golden chariot. In the back behind tinted windows like a little celebrity.

"He seems to be pretty calm now."

Mabel glanced at the baby in her rearview mirror.

"Trust me. He's a terror."

I shifted the box in my arms.

"Mabel, it's okay. I don't mind the crying. The diapers or whatever, it's no big deal."

My sister shook her head.

"Fern, I'm telling you no."

Was Mabel scared I'd hurt the baby? Cast a dangerous spell? Or was Mabel hiding something she didn't want me to see?

"Anyway, thanks again for picking up the box. We'll do lunch sometime."

"Right. Sure. Lunch."

She pulled into the garage.

One day outside with Rose, she brushes against my trunk.

"How's about that box of your mother's things? Opened it up yet?" Rose and her zebra puppet, Zack, waiting for an answer. Rose shakes his black yarn mane like he is getting impatient.

"No, not yet."

"Why? Are you scared?"

I make it like I'm going back inside like I have something to do. Rose stops me with her words.

"What if we open it together?"

Strangely enough, I brought my car keys for whatever reason. Maybe the reason is this. Maybe now is the time. I unlock my trunk. Take out the hefty box. Rose points the way with Zack.

"Let's take the box to the gazebo!"

When you're in the gazebo, everyone watches you. Why is that person out there? Whatever are they doing? No one ever sits there because everybody looks. A Panopticon effect of the All-Seeing Eye. But I say okay. After all, it's Rose.

In the gazebo are cracked plastic chairs and crusty buckets of rock salt. I place the box in the center. Cast a circle around us. On the fly, think of a spell to guide us through the opening:

Let whatever comes out, not harm. Let whatever not harm, come in.

"Let's open it already!" Rose kneels on the boards, removing Zack from her hand. Edges her fingernail beneath a strip of tape. Gives the tape a yank. It comes off in a zip. I unfold the flaps. My mother's iron cauldron is on the very top. Upside down with its three short legs sticking up like antlers. Rose hoists the heavy cauldron and dons it as a helmet.

"Rose! Stop! No! That is not a toy!"

"I know, I know. It's a witch's pot, isn't it?"

"It's called a cauldron."

"Is it cursed?"

"No, it isn't cursed but it bears my mother's energy."

Rose removes the cauldron and stations it beside her.

"That thing is really heavy!"

"I'm amazed you were able to lift it."

"Must be magic!" Rose says. "Maybe I'm a witch!"

In a gust, the wind picks up and shifts a

plastic chair. It glides a few inches across the boards as if pushed by a hand.

"Whoa, that was weird," says Rose.

Very *wyrd* indeed.

"Hey, is that a wand?"

My mother's wand is ash wood. About a foot long and two inches wide. A simple tool she whittled herself. I present the wand to Rose.

"Can you do magic with that?"

"It isn't like a magician's wand tapping on a hat and making a bunny appear. It's for shifting energy. When you're not using it, it goes on your altar."

"Like the altar at church?"

"Similar."

Rose gives a little nod.

I reach across Rose and put the wand in the cauldron.

"I know what that is!" Rose says. "It's called a chalice. It's the thing Jesus drank out of with his disciples. It turned wine into blood during the Last Supper."

Another tool Ma carved. Turned, the proper term for the crafting of cups from wood. She had a shed with a lathe of which she was very proud.

"The chalice symbolizes the feminine."

"What's that mean?"

"Feminine means women."

"But Jesus was a man. How come he had a chalice?"

I rack my brain to think of a thoughtful answer. In a blink, it doesn't matter.

Rose has already moved on.

"Oooh, a knife!"

"This is called an athame."

"It doesn't look sharp. How's it supposed to cut anything?"

Rose pushes hair from her eyes.

"It isn't used for cutting. Not like a kitchen knife. This goes on your altar too and is used in rituals. It has two sides that symbolize the feminine and masculine. Masculine means men."

Harder than I thought to explain masculine and feminine. I'm not happy with my explanations—they're much too simplistic—but I am talking to a kid.

Rose lets out a big yawn and says her tummy's growling.

"Don't you want to see the last tool?"

Rose runs out of the gazebo, breaking through the circle, a no-no when it comes to the spirit world. But what can I do? Not all is in my power. Chicken nuggets and television were calling Rose's name.

The last thing in the box is my mother's Book of Shadows. I carefully remove it. Hold it out in my hands. A witch's Book of Shadows is her most personal tool. It includes spells she's written and tried; notes on how the spells manifested. It might include 'recipes' from her particular practice. Poultices, tinctures, teas— how did they turn out?

I bring the tome close to me. Run my hand over the cover, a nubby maroon felt. The latch is a strap of leather hooked over an amethyst.

Now I'm tempted to look.

The first pages are spells written when my mother was a young witch. Before she had me and Mabel. To think of my mother, young.

Next, is a recipe for an herbal tea. Ma listed the ingredients, but some are blurred. Looks like she spilled the very tea she was trying to make.

A recipe for a poultice of Chaga mushrooms.

A soak for menstrual cramps based on the moon cycle.

What secrets were in these pages,

hundreds and hundreds of them? What knowledge, or what powers, had my mother left for me?

I close the book. Give the cover three knocks. Draw up the circle. Bring the box inside.

And as I do, the prickling awareness I am being watched. Curtains quickly closed. The lowering of blinds. Mr. C? Not-Reba? Slippers with her Cyclops? Faces I cannot see?

Who was watching me?

Inside, I place my mother's Book of Shadows on my altar. My altar is positioned in the Eastern corner of my unit, facing the rising sun. Symbolizing hope. It is nothing fancy. Stacked milk crates, a wooden board across, hidden by a floral cloth draping to the floor. I arrange the tools my mother left behind.

But something is missing. What's missing is my mother. How to communicate with Ma? I needed a scrying mirror. In the bedroom, I remove the veil from my mirror. There I am. Take it down off the wall.

A trip to the hardware store to buy a can of black paint. An old bed sheet to serve as my drop cloth. A brush I had saved from my painting days. A shooing away of Chance who wanted to participate. No, Chance, don't step in the paint. No black kitty paw prints.

Painting is a process.

I paint my mirror black and wait for it to dry. This takes several days but I must be patient. Lust for result, it's called, when you focus too much on the goal and not on the magic itself.

Finally, the mirror is ready. I'm ready to speak to Ma.

"Hey, Ma, can I ask you something?"

My mother nods.

"Did you send Rose to me to snap me out of my funk?"

You give me too much credit, Fern. I was never that good a witch.

"You were in my eyes, Ma."

Perception is everything.

"You got that right. Lately, I've been feeling like I'm falling short. Like I'm not the witch I was meant to be."

Your authentic witch, you mean.

"Right, my authentic witch."

Sometimes we get sidetracked. Frankly, I can't believe it when I look back at my life. How was I a witch for seventy years?

Ma sips something.

"Are you having coffee?"

No, it's this AfterLife tea. Gosh, I wish you could try it.

My lip trembles.

Now, Fern, don't you cry.

"I really miss you, Ma! Me and Mabel—"

I know. You and your sister don't get along.

"We used to though, didn't we?"

You did when you were kids.

"What happened? Why are we so distant? I feel like if we were closer, maybe I wouldn't be struggling."

Marriage, Fern, Marriage. Marriage pulls siblings apart. Unfortunately, things have unfolded as they have. Believe me, it's not what I had envisioned for my daughters.

"Mark is such an asshole! Sorry, but he is!"

Honey, I'm in the afterlife. Nothing offends me anymore. Not that it did when I was alive either.

I laugh and it comes out sad.

"I'm ashamed to say this, Ma, but I wish I were dead. With you in the spirit realm. It sounds so much better there!"

Please don't envy me, Fern. Your life is so very precious. You have a purpose, you do. It's just not clear to you yet.

"I'm trying, Ma. I'm trying."

I brush away a tear.

"What I was saying was—wait, what was I saying?"

About Mabel.

"Oh right. Her being distant. I mean, I sort of get it. Mabel got the life she wanted. The big house, the husband, the baby. Living on the rich side of Baronsville. But why is she so cold to me? What did I do to deserve it?"

You called out her husband, remember? How he treated you at the barbecue?

"Wait. You *knew* about the barbecue incident?"

Ma shifts. It sounds like ruffling feathers.

"Do you have wings or something?"

Not wings, exactly. More like energy fields.

I focus on them.

"They look yellowish."

On my end, they're marigold.

Ma and her marigolds. Every summer she'd plant them around our mailbox. Marigolds were strong, sturdy, and could hold up to any conditions. Much like my mother herself. Ma wasn't a shrinking violet.

And neither are you, Fern. You're the stronger daughter. Just don't tell Mabel I told you.

"Don't worry, Ma. We don't talk anymore."

Ma sighs the breath of dreams.

The thing about being a spirit is, that it doesn't give me answers. Human behavior is as mysterious to me as ever.

"You're saying it's up to me to figure things out with Mabel."

Ma's light begins to shrink.

"Ma, you still there?"

Dimmer, dimmer, dark.

I've lost the frequency.

Mark harassed me once. Shoulder to shoulder at the barbecue when he and Mabel were only dating. A comment on his penis length huffed into my ear. I turned away my head, as in leave me alone. Then I heard something else:

"Don't be a cold fish."

I took my paper plate and found the condiments table, squirting Heinz ketchup on an empty bun. I'd left my dog on the grill.

That night, I tossed and turned. Should I tell my sister? What if she married this man? Shouldn't she know beforehand what type of person he was? She should, was my decision. I called her on the phone. Early next day, first thing. To clear my mind, my conscience. I told her what had happened exactly as it happened.

Mabel dismissed my concern.

"Ever heard of a joke?"

A long pause.

"Mabel, I'm sorry, a *joke*? Did you not hear what I said?"

"I did and I'm telling you: you need to lighten up."

"*Lighten up*? But Mark—"

"Fern, the problem is you. You're seeing things all wrong. Mark is the man I'm marrying."

Mabel ended the call.

In a flash, it all became clear: Mabel would betray me. To win the husband's prize, she'd do whatever it took. Distance herself from the weird witch sister didn't fit her image. Her newer, richer image ascending the social ladder.

I represented her past.

A past she had erased.

And yet, I loved my sister, missed her more than ever, and often thought of the times we had shared as kids. Playing in the woods. Catching frogs. Toads. Concocting spells like our mother. For Ma had raised us witch. Raised us to be witches. But that was not the path my sister chose to take. I had to accept her choice. It was not to be.

Still, how Ma would flip us to check our scalps at night. For ticks, those tiny vampires. "Come here girls, let's check." Feel with spider fingers for what drew blood and bloated.

I wish we were young again.

"All set, girls. You're good."

I like Sundays like this. Everybody's home doing whatever they're doing. Watching television. Drinking. Sleeping. A big part of this peacefulness is due to the quarry's closed, also the firing range. A reprieve from the sound of blasted rocks and rounds of fired ammo. And yet my ears are ringing like tiny distant bells. I've never known what's it like to hear nothing at all.

I think it must be nice to hear nothing at all.

But where is Rose? She usually comes around to visit. Show me a new puppet friend. Or to say hello to Chance. Startle him, scaredy cat! The thump of her boots on my porch, her rosy face at the window, my doorbell ringing, ringing.

The complex is too quiet.

I zipper up my coat. Head across the street. Maybe she's playing here? Over here on the snowbank? By the fence around the quarry?

This cannot be real.

I'm looking through the slats. I'm seeing Rose's body. Upon the granite rocks, twisted and contorted, way down at the bottom, deep down in the pit. Her pink snowsuit lay still.

I let out a scream.

I'm positive I'm screaming but no one seems to hear me. How come no one hears me? I turn in the direction of the complex. Vultures on the roof.

How can this be happening?

Look again through the slats. Rose's body is positioned beside a piece of machinery. Piles of granite around her waiting to be removed. Go get her grandmother. Now. Run back across the street. Bang on her door. Barely get the words out. Nonna dials from a rotary phone pressing a finger to her ear. In the background her TV drones like it's a regular day. A commercial for Metamucil to unplug your bowels. Now with Vitamin D added for an immunity boost.

Nonna is wearing a housedress. Her hair is a fright wig. Flat patch where her skull was pressed against her recliner. Everywhere, stuff. Figurines. Tchotchkes. Footstools. Lamps. Four vacuums. A headboard for a queen-sized bed. An upright piano with a microwave on it. Magazines. Newspapers. A narrow path to the kitchen between tall stacks of boxes. You'd have to walk it sideways with arms pressed to your sides. Hoping not to fall.

"The ambulance is coming."

No coat, no shoes, Nonna thunders out. Next, I'd see her bare feet squatting next to Rose, heels tucked under her rear like she was genuflecting. Shape folding over shape like a closing flower. Larger petals over smaller ones. Grandmother over granddaughter.

I stand along the rock face as Nonna inspects Rose. "Rose, can you hear me? It's Nonna." No answer. Again, she asks can you hear me, gently squeezing Rose's arm. The squishy sound of her snowsuit carries on the wind. I must look away. It all ends here at the quarry. That's why they put us here. They wanted poor people to die.

The only neighbor who will speak to me is Peter. I find him on his porch repairing an old Schwinn. Peter is wearing a nice coat he got from Goodwill. Heavy and filled with down, such coats do not run cheap. He's sitting on an overturned bucket perfect for the height of repair.

"Peter, talk to me. Tell me what's going on."

Peter reaches for a rag. "Nice day we're having. The sky is still dark. Seems to be the way this winter."

"Come on, Peter. You know me."

Peter keeps his head down as he greases a chain. "I'm sorry, Fern. It hurts my heart to say this. But the neighbors are saying things."

"Aren't I a good person? Didn't I come and check on you that time in the rain?"

Peter raises his eyes over his John Lennon glasses.

"They're saying that—well. That you're an outcast, Fern. You don't belong with the rest of us. Being a witch and all."

"So that automatically means I'm responsible for what happened to Rose? It's crazy, Peter! It's nonsense! Can't you see? They're making a scapegoat of me!"

Peter tests the tires. "The whole thing is a mess."

Even here with Peter, I feel I'm being watched. And Peter senses it too. He keeps dropping the air pump. Then Peter says the thing I worried he would say.

"It's—" He gazes into spokes. "It's not a normal thing for adults to befriend kids."

"If they're not their kids," he adds. "It's not the world we're in."

"But Rose was like family to me—like the daughter I never had!"

Peter grabs hold of a pedal and slowly rotates the wheel. Something about it isn't right. He searches in his toolbox for the wrench he needs. Rattle. Clank. Click. Found it.

"Peter, you've got to believe me. I didn't do this to Rose!"

But I can see it happening, the shutting down of me. The changing of the channel. The closing of a window. All's been said.

There's nothing more to say.

Nightmares.

Five faces in a ring. Mr. C. Not-Reba. Slippers. Peter. Nonna. Rope binds me to an ash tree. A hand strikes a match. Flame shoots like a star. I burst into a blaze.

A crumpled, fallen bird at the bottom of the quarry. Vultures are pick, pick, picking. Eating Rose before me. I scream and no one hears.

I sink quickly as death. Above me, through the water, I can hear them cheering. Strangers on the shoreline, there to watch me drown.

I'm chased down Quarry Street by someone I can't see. I hear a gun go off. I feel the blast in my spine. I fall into the quarry. I never hit the bottom.

The cop who questions me is Officer Daly. Immediately I think of the cop in grade school who taught us about drugs. His name was Officer Daly, too. Maybe this is his son. The original Officer Daly passed around a teddy bear. Said instead of taking drugs, hug your teddy bear. We all got a bear at fifth-grade graduation. In sixth grade, kids threw away the bears, partied, and did drugs. Wore D.A.R.E. shirts ironically like singers in punk rock bands.

"Mind if I come inside to ask you a few questions?"

The officer is a child. Can't be more than twenty-two years old. A baby-faced white boy growing into his uniform. Regardless, he's packing heat. Look at the size of that gun.

"We can talk right here on my porch. Here, I've got two chairs."

Officer Daly refuses the moldy plastic chair I took out of the gazebo. If he's standing, I'm standing. A cop is not above me.

Every question comes with an implication. Are you the mother of the child? (No.) Are you married? (No.) Do you have any children of your own? (No.) How did you know Rose? (She helped me clean off my car.) Were you being paid to watch her? (No.)

"I've spoken to your neighbors, and they say you are a witch. Can you confirm this?"

A pause.

"I don't see what my being a witch has to do with anything. A little girl has died. Isn't that more important?"

He scribbles in his notebook.

I'm about to say I'm not obligated to answer any more of your questions. Hadn't I already given him a detailed account of what happened? When I look down at his pocket. A red cherry, poking out. Rose's sundae hat. Evidence, collected.

Sharp pain in my chest.

I cannot bring back Rose no matter what I say. No spell, no incantation, no ritual, no vision. Rose was gone, gone. My magic had its limits.

"Officer Daly, I know how it looks. But everything, in reality, is not what it seems."

With a snap, he closes his notebook. Pockets his blue pen.

"Thank you for your time. We'll call if we have any more questions."

▼

A van from News Channel 4 is parked outside my unit. Night and day, it's there. I wait until the cover of darkness to throw out the trash. A news reporter appears and accosts me. I recognize her from TV.

Lisa Romero in a bright yellow coat emblazoned with the station's logo. The intrusion of the media sears like a blazing fire. A microphone shoved in my face.

"Excuse me, are you Fern?"

Everyone knew about the story. A little girl died at the quarry and a witch had stood accused. Wouldn't that be great for ratings?

"Can I ask you some questions?"

I pitch my trash in the dumpster and when I turn around, an entire film crew is set up in a matter of seconds. A sound guy. A lighting person. Camera person, rolling. And Lisa Romero, the famed reporter who did these sorts of stories.

Sensational. Controversial. In your neighborhood. Stories to fill the time between local traffic and weather. A girl died at the quarry, a possible victim of witchcraft. Three minutes to get a rise. Now it's time for sports.

"No comment," I say, head down. Lisa chases me like an animal. My unit seems so far away and yet I've got to get there. I need safety, shelter. To get away from this.

"You don't care the little girl died?"

I stop in my tracks. The camera swoops around to get a better shot. Light in my eyes. A giant fuzzy caterpillar floats above my head. And Lisa's face of makeup, pancake thick and fake.

"Rose was my friend," I say. "She was a wonderful kid."

Lisa presses me further.

"That's all you have to say?"

Did I have more to say? I look up at the roof. One vulture. Only one today? How we counted vultures, played with hand puppets, and listened to pretend hearts. All of that over, a dream. And all of this is surreal.

"Surely you must know what people are saying about you. That it was you who made Rose fall. Did you cast some sort of spell? Aren't you a witch?"

I can't do this. I can't. I can't defend myself.

I raise my hand to the camera and push my body through the crush. Forge ahead. Flee.

"Excuse me, I have to go."

My sister's Chevy Tahoe drives up Quarry Street. Mabel, predictably, has come to take a look.

Everyone has heard. Everybody knows.

Faster than wildfire did the story spread. Lisa Romero's news report certainly didn't help. But also, it's a thing about Baronsville. A big town but it's small in that it is divided. Doesn't take long for rumors to jump from one side to the other.

Worse than rumors, accusations. That I had been the one who did it. Killed Rose and cast a spell.

I'm scared to leave my unit.

At the kitchen window, I hear a rumble of an engine. It has to be her Tahoe. I knew my sister's car. And there it drove past the quarry, pausing for a good long look. Can you see through the fence? Down to the spot she died? Any blood on the rocks?

The quarry is a tourist site.

Cadillacs. Mercedes. Teslas. Lexuses. Driving through on day trips. Like those drive-through zoos where you keep your windows up. When no one cared before what happened at the complex, now everybody did. Got themselves involved. From the rich side of

Baronsville drove in curious residents. Gawking. Staring. Pointing.

The tragedy is everyone's business.

I cannot live like this. Holed up in my unit. Running out of groceries, I missed the donation day. Once a week, that's it. And poor Chance. Eating cans of cat food, which he didn't even like. The backup cans for snowstorms.

My cell phone rings.

"Fern? It's Mabel."

"Mabel? I was just—I think I see your car."

"Yes, that's me."

My sister is drinking something. Sound of a pulled-back lid. Likely macchiato.

"I'm pulled over across your street because it's got me thinking."

"Thinking? About what?"

"You and this whole Rose thing."

This was my sister: sudden. We hadn't spoken since Ma's death. She'd start right here, right now, with whatever she had to say. That's one way we were different. I ruminated. Obsessed. Thought things over and over. Mabel thought like an arrow. Shot her shot. Done.

"Mabel, would you like to come in? I

mean, you're right here."

"No, that's okay. Sort of in a rush."

Always in a rush—another way we were different. I could stare at a tree for the entirety of an afternoon. Schedules hated me. Mabel was in love with them.

"So, here's what I was thinking. Mark, the baby, and I are going to be away. We need someone to housesit. I was thinking maybe you?"

"Housesit?"

"It would be for a week. I realize it's short notice, but hubs got a good deal on airline tickets. Figured it was time for a break from all the Baronsville madness. Frankly, we're over it."

She sighs into the phone.

"I've never housesat before. What is it I have to do?"

"Not much really. Just make it seem like there are people inside. Living and breathing. Making noise. That sort of thing."

"Basically, be a body."

"Exactly, be a body."

Be a body. Something I can do. About the level of achievement I can expect from my downhill life. *Here lies a body. That's all she ever was.*

"I'll pay you, of course. How's a thousand dollars sound?"

I nearly drop my phone.

"A *thousand* dollars?"

"Bit on the low side but I'd rather have a family member do it than a random stranger. Family discount, right?"

"Right, family discount."

I don't know what I'm saying. Repeating whatever Mabel says because she says it with confidence. Mabel knows what she's doing. Clearly, I do not.

"Plus, with everything going on with you..."

"How did—"

"Look Fern, I know what happened. The entire town of Baronsville does. The problem should blow over soon. Just need to give it time."

The problem. Mabel whose only problem was finding a sitter for her McMansion. Imagine your only problem was finding a sitter for your McMansion.

"I mean, it's a shame, *of course,* it's a shame the little girl died at the quarry. But where was the little girl's mother when all of this was happening?"

"Her mother—"

Disappeared?

Vanished without a trace?

Moved away somewhere?

"Rose lived with her grandmother."

"There you go! Explains it right there, doesn't it? This is why poor people shouldn't be having children."

I don't know what to say. Except I needed an out. And here it was, an out. Housesitting for my sister. For the first time since Rose died, I'm starting to feel a bit lighter.

I'm disgusted at myself for feeling a bit lighter.

"Listen to what I'm saying, Fern. This has nothing to do with you. If you'd get outside of your head for a second, you'd see the bigger picture."

"The bigger picture?"

"Are you her mother? No. You're not her grandmother, either. None of this, and I mean *none of this*, has anything to do with you."

Mabel is buttering me up because she wants me to housesit. Fine. I could use a buttering. Lately, I'd been a dried, grisly chicken carcass rotting on my couch. Not going anywhere. Wishing I was dead. Barring that, an escape from the complex. The eyes were too much on me. The rumors swirling. The Tempest. Not to mention, a thousand dollars? I needed the money.

"Can I take Chance with me?"

"Hold on." She puts down her cup. "That's fine. As long you keep him to a room and not running around the whole house."

How would Mabel know if I let Chance run free? Then I remembered: cameras. Mabel had the WatchMyHome app. Wherever they were going, she'd be watching me.

"Yes. I'll do it."

"You will? Great! So glad you can help. I'll be in touch when the time gets closer. You know, to give you the key code."

"Sure. Um, hey Mabel?"

"Hmm?"

"Do you miss Ma?"

I hear her tapping the wheel.

"Sometimes."

"Just sometimes? Because I miss her a lot. I feel like it happened so fast."

"It's not like it was a shock. You had to have known it was coming. Ma's health had been failing for a long time."

I think of our walk around the lake, Ma's memory receding.

"She was only in the nursing home for what was it, a year?"

"I know, Fern, but that's what happens. These places speed up death."

Speed up death. What a thing to say. Mabel has no filter, she prides herself on honesty, and the sad thing is, she's right. These places speed up death. Maybe that was my problem, I needed less of a filter. Needed to drop the veil.

"Did we do all we could for Ma?"

"Yes, we did. You have to stop blaming yourself."

Easy for Mabel to say. I had been close with Ma in a way my sister wasn't. In short, I was a witch. My sister was not.

We were of two worlds: the spiritual and the mundane.

Mabel was a dietician until she met her husband. Measuring out portions. Counting calories. That's how Mabel saw the world—her view of it was fixed—while mine my liquid, mutable. Everything is in flux.

I want to say goodbye, thanks for calling me, but Mabel ends the call, doesn't spare the chance. And there it goes, her Tahoe, quickly driving off. I pet Chance. He purrs.

"Looks like we're going on a trip."

Mabel's foyer is a cavern. White vaulted ceiling. A geometric gold chandelier hanging in front of a window. The window is a half-circle like a sun rising on the horizon. You cannot reach the rising sun unless on a very tall ladder. That or one of those Genies I've seen in arenas. Probably could fit in here if the door was a bit bigger. A guy up in the bucket who is not afraid of heights. Hanging pennants from the rafters. Division 1 State Champs.

The half-sun window is sparkling. How many birds have died thinking it clear passage? The wooden beams are exposed like a barn. On such beams would a flying free bird love to perch herself—until she learns the portal isn't clear at all. The pain is clear and stunning. It's the shock of the thing that kills. Not the actual impact.

I bring Chance in his crate and set him on the hardwood. I double-dosed him with KittyCalm before we left the house, assuming he'd freak when he saw the scale of Mabel's. Wheel in my roller bag. Set it next to his crate.

Mabel's kitchen looks like something out of a magazine. The countertop is granite from the quarry. Mabel said when she had the house built that everything would be 'custom'.

Boasting that the materials to build the house would be locally sourced. I wondered which quarry explosion produced this countertop. A ceramic basket of apples is arranged into a tower. Arrange, arranged, arrangement. Mabel's life was all these things. Curated to the point you were scared to breathe.

A screen on their fridge lights up. Just as I suspected. Half-empty condiment bottles. A random thing of salsa. Search their cabinets. Oatmeal. Soup. Pasta. Sauce. Okay, at least there's *something*. But what did these people *eat*? Guess they ordered takeout. Or one of those meal prep services my sister recommended back when she was working as a dietician.

The kitchen is frighteningly clean. Antiseptically spotless. No evidence of a baby. No jam splatters. No stains. No highchair in sight. Must have stashed it away. Mabel was hell-bent on not letting the baby disrupt her life. The baby would be an addition, like a shiny appliance. Their house would look exactly as it was. It wouldn't show signs of change.

Return to the foyer.

"Well Chance, there's cans of tuna. You're

gonna eat like a king." I peek into his crate. Check his belly for up and down movement. Good. Didn't overdose him. "Let's see where our room is."

Chance lets out a weak meow.

It echoes loud as a roar.

Carefully carry his crate up the grand staircase. The staircase is floating steel planks ascending the length of the wall, leading to a balcony overlooking the foyer. Step by step, plank by plank—I'm getting vertigo. As it was, my antidepressants led to bouts of dizziness. Don't look down. The only way up is up.

Come upon a hallway. The first door is the guest bathroom. The wall of the standing shower is granite from the quarry. Not smooth tiles, the granite's roughhewn. A replica of the rockface. The sink's a granite slab mounted on a pedestal. The faucet doesn't have handles. The water runs with a swipe. Calibrates the temperature according to your own.

"This must be the guest bedroom."

Mabel made it welcoming in an Airbnb sort of way. A wooden hamper of rolled towels was placed askew on the bed. A Mason jar of wildflowers on the nightstand. Mabel and her Mason jars. Had them at her wedding, too. The comforter is gray. I flip over the tag: Nest Organic Bedding. I never shopped at Nest on her side of town. Five hundred dollars for a pillowcase was considered a bargain.

Nowhere are pictures of the family. Nowhere are pictures of the baby. Not in the guest bedroom. Not in the hall. Not downstairs. This place could be anywhere. In-home security cameras are strategically placed to get wide shots of rooms. Digital eyes high in corners like ravens atop busts.

I open Chance's crate. Poor little guy. Totters out. Lowers himself. Roosts like a hen. "Take it easy, Chance." I close the door behind me. I want to see where it is they keep the baby.

The nursery room looks nothing at all like a nursery room. A crib and a changing table are the only indications. But even the crib and changing table look like adult furniture, like geometric minimalist consoles. The walls are Pelican Gray. I remember Mabel telling me this: "We've decided to go with Pelican Gray for the baby's room." No colorful mobiles. No cute art on the walls. Not even stuffed animals. A granite cylinder on the changing table dispenses baby wipes.

I sit in a modern version of a rocking chair. All straight and narrow. Imagine feeding a baby like this. Rocking into the night. I said from the start I didn't want children. As in prove me wrong. Show me I want children. The universe had shrugged its shoulders. Fine, you don't want children. Took the wheel and drove me to Planned Parenthood.

I close my eyes. Rock. Envision me as a mother. What would my life have been if I didn't have an abortion?

I went to a Planned Parenthood in an industrial complex. Cookie cutter loading docks with semi-trucks backed up to them. Each dock had its own office for drivers to report. Say I'm here with delivery from such and such a place.

Next door to Planned Parenthood was a company called AeroWare Dynamics. I wondered what they made as I parked and went inside. Something for air conditioners, maybe.

What I saw inside the waiting room I had seen before. In a rerun of a sitcom, I recognized the set. A mix of maroons and browns, beige carpeting, and dark red cushioned chairs. Television from the nineties: a monolithic block of a screen inside a wooden cabinet. Playing was one of those good morning shows where all the dolled-up women laugh. How can they be so happy? Producers must feed them alcohol by the gallon. A potted plant on the coffee table turned out to be real. To evaluate it, I pressed my nail through its verdant flesh. Sorry plant, forgive me. Didn't mean to hurt you.

I felt for plants. They kept us alive.

Pamphlets spread on the table for you to

read. Options for contraceptives. What to do if you've been raped. What to do if you're pregnant and don't want to be. Poster versions hanging on the walls.

Beside me was a couple waiting for the same thing. It came in their collective aura. Fear of the unknown. A difficult decision. Didn't have to say a word, I knew why they were there. During the time we waited, I listened to them talking. Mostly they were talking about the new stadium. How the man thought maybe he could get a job there. How the woman thought that would be good if he could get a job there.

I thought because they'd gotten there first, they'd have their abortion first.

I was proven wrong: they took us in together.

It went smoother than I expected. The first day and the second day after, cramping like PMS. My body was sore and tired. I slept. Then on the third day, I started bleeding profusely. Thought the toilet I sat on would overflow with blood.

Called an Uber to take me to the hospital. Towels stuffed between my thighs like a puff-a-lump. The driver laid down plastic sheets reserved for nightclub goers, their vomit, and bodily fluids like extra passengers. "No worries. That's why I've got the plastic." Ushering in my bags, he gently closed the door.

Thank you, Uber driver. You've given me hope in men.

Unlike the male doctor in the emergency room whose attitude was one of general annoyance. "Didn't you have an abortion?" Yes, I had an abortion—that's what I told the nurse—but my body won't stop bleeding.

"There's nothing I can do."

Nothing he could do. Wasn't he a doctor? I'm here on a gurney, bleeding. I can barely walk. My cramps are sharp as daggers.

"You'll have to wait it out."

He chalked it off as hormones. A recalibration of imbalances following my abortion. The bleeding should stop eventually. Go home and take Tylenol. Here's a prescription for high-dose iron pills. Don't want you getting anemic.

Back home, I soaked in the tub, holding the safety handles. I focused on the good. The driver who had helped me. And not so much the bad. The doctor who couldn't be bothered.

I sunk down to my shoulders. The water

rose to my neck. I dipped my chin and opened my mouth to wet my bottom lip. My teeth like a waterline, I would sink no further.

Astride the faucet, my feet appeared at a distance. How strange was the human body? Bones and nails and teeth and flesh and feet on which we walked. I counted my ten toes, the nails of them like moons.

A chain attached to the plug like an anchor in an ocean.

I gripped the chain, tugging to test its strength, attempting to dislodge the plug without the use of my hands. And when I did, searing pain shot up my inner thighs. What did toes have to do with thighs? What did the moon, the tides? What did the stars, our births?

Everything.

My body was a cosmos. A constellation of symptoms. Physical pain like comets coursing through my system. Twenty years? A lifetime? How long did comets orbit?

In the water, my blood swirled.

On the sink, a candle burned.

In the morning at my sister's, a ringing doorbell wakes me. I'm in an utter fog having taken three sleeping pills. Chance is cleaning himself at the foot of the bed. The doorbell rings again. I check my phone: 9:00 A.M. I find my way downstairs, splaying my hands against the wall as there is no railing. The last thing I need is to die falling off Mabel's staircase.

I open the door, shield my eyes, and squint. Matchstick body. Lollypop head. Big black almond eyes. Backlit by a glowing spaceship or maybe it's the sun.

"Excuse me," says the alien. "Didn't know they were having guests."

"I'm her sister, Fern. I'm housesitting for the week. The three of them are away."

"Oh? Mabel didn't tell me they were going on vacation. Well, I came to tell them a strange car was parked in front of their house."

The alien glances over her shoulder at my beater.

"That's my car."

"And who did you say you were?"

"Her sister, Fern. I'm sorry, and who are you?"

"I'm Terry, your sister's best friend. I live across the street."

I look across at Terry's house. It's the mirror image of Mabel's. Down to the barn doors and the rooster weathervane. What was it with rich people and their love of rural aesthetics?

Terry looks me up and down.

"You look nothing like her."

"Funny thing is, I used to. Then Mabel got plastic surgery and turned into someone else."

"That's really none of my business."

"No, of course not. Just saying."

This Terry woman. Shriveled raisin face like an octogenarian, although she wasn't old. Early 40s? And what they called 'the ladder', considered the crowning achievement of dieting, when the bones between the breasts showed themselves like rungs. A low-cut shirt and yoga pants. Wasn't Terry cold?

"It's just very strange, that's all. Mabel didn't say anything about their going away. And Mabel tells me everything."

"I don't know what to tell you."

"No worries, I'll text Mabel. See how she's doing with Mark and the baby and everything. Maybe I can help somehow."

"Have a nice day, Terry."

I swiftly close the door.

A sweep of fur around my heels, a meow that means good morning.

Mabel texts immediately: "Please keep Chance upstairs!"

I reply: "K."

Give the camera a wave.

In preparation for our stay, Mabel bought Chance a robotic litter box. I've seen these things on Amazon. Watched the demonstration videos. Apparently with iLitter you never had to clean your litter box ever again. Had this raking motion activated by sensors, scraped away the clumps to be disintegrated by lasers. I set it up in the guest bathroom and begged Chance to use it.

"Please Chance, I know it's weird. Just poop in the thing, okay?"

I hear Chance in there now doing his business. iLitter is cheering him on. *Good job! Nice work! Way to go, kitty!* Why must everything come with positive affirmations?

Toxic optimism. Down to litter boxes.

Already I'm worried when we get home, Chance won't use his regular litter box. Too much of a dopamine hit with this one. He'll never return to reality.

Then I think: so, what? I'm taking this fancy box with me. At home, let it cheer on Chance.

He's a good boy. Deserves it.

▼

I watch a lot of television.

I don't have cable at home and Mabel has all the channels. Over a thousand. I get stuck on the gardening network for something like six hours. Fall down the rabbit hole of a marathon of *Ground Coverage*, the series where couples debate what kind of ground coverage they should get. A horticulturist and couples therapist walk them through the process. In the end, they choose pachysandra and start having sex again.

Terry texted Mabel as she said she would. For the next morning, her attitude has done a complete turnaround. It's like we're best friends, like we've known each other for years.

Terry smiles, showing herself in.

"I brought you some groceries!"

Terry puts the bag on the kitchen island and begins to unpack, presenting each item like Vanna White.

"Let's start with the good stuff—ice cream!"

Terry holds up a pint of something called Chocolate Magnum. It has a golden lid like a luxury item. Terry shelves it in the freezer.

"And I got you frozen pizzas." Another brand I never buy because they're too expensive: Great Wolf Lodge. We lived in New Jersey, Home of the 'World's Best Pizza', yet some lodge in Montana claimed it held the prize.

Terry stashes the pizzas in the freezer, then rolls up the grocery bag and stores it under the counter. Already knows where the bag's supposed to go. Probably in the same cabinet as her own McMansion. Terry pops a pod in the Keurig.

"Can I make you a coffee?"

"No, that's okay. I don't drink coffee."

"Don't drink coffee? How do you *live*?"

Terry slides onto a stool and waits for her mug to fill. I'm standing with my back to the farmhouse sink, arms crossed against my chest. I guess this is what they did every day. Terry came over and helped herself to coffee and offered my sister a cup. I've stepped into the role of Mabel like an understudy.

"Mabel tells me you're a witch!"

"Yes, that's correct."

"Do you wear a pointy hat?"

Terry mimes it on her head.

"The thing about the pointy hat is a stereotype. Not everyone who's a witch wears the pointy hat."

"You don't wear the hat?"

"No, I don't wear the hat."

I wonder if Terry knows our mother was a witch. Probably not. *Definitely* not. Mabel was ashamed of her past. Wanted to pretend she fell out of the sky and landed in this house. A house she built from scratch like her brand-new life.

"I think it's great," says Terry. "Witches are really *in* these days. It's cool your sister's got one. Wish I had one myself."

Terry studies the Keurig's last drips.

"Sure you don't want anything? I think there's tea in the cabinet."

"No, that's okay."

"Suit yourself."

With the mug filled, Terry takes a sip. "Please. Sit. You're making me nervous standing over there."

I take a seat on a metal stool, hard and uncomfortable. What happened to kitchen tables? Regular chairs with pads? They all decided their kitchens should look like Starbucks.

"I'd love to hear more about this witch thing."

"You mean witchcraft? There's a lot to say about it. It's not something you can go through quickly. It honestly takes a lifetime."

"Just give me the basics. A set of bullet points. Here, I'll help you start. Do you have a cauldron?"

I want to give Terry the boot, but she brought me groceries. Plus, any rudeness to Terry would be reported to Mabel. My pay would be docked, no doubt. Guess I must answer.

"Yes, I have a cauldron."

"What about a cat?"

"Yes. He's here upstairs in fact."

Terry takes a sip.

"How about murdering children?"

A beat.

"Little joke there, Fern. I know what you're going through at the complex."

She pats me on the knee.

I get up off the stool. "Thanks for the groceries, Terry."

"I'm sorry, did I offend you?"

"Frankly? Yes, you did. What happened to Rose isn't funny."

"I didn't say it was funny."

"You said it was a joke."

Terry trembles like a fly stuck in a spider web. Am I scaring Terry? Good. Let her be scared. She had it coming. And more.

"Now if you'll excuse me, I have things to do. You know where the door is. You can see yourself out."

Terry reaches for my arm as I leave the kitchen. My voice raises to a yell as I throw her off.

"I'm telling you to leave!"

"Fern, please! I wasn't—I didn't mean anything by it!"

A burning deep inside. A fury too hot to take. Always the same, always the same. Burning witches at the stake. My anger overwhelms me.

Back upstairs, I rage.

Hurl the comforter off the bed. Smash the Mason jar of flowers. Scattered petals, soggy, in a pool of water, spreading. What else can I throw?

There goes the basket of towels.

The camera blinks. Zooms. My sister Mabel, watching. Welcome to my life. This hell of no escape. Damned. Doomed. Cursed.

Chance runs off, screeching.

A flash of Rose's body at the bottom of the quarry. Twisted. Contorted. Pink.

I collapse on the stripped bed.

The bowl of the sky goes dark like in a movie theater. One moon appears. Then another. Moons of different sizes and luminosities fill the entire sky. I look over at my mother. We are standing in an open field. We hear the booming voice of a movie director. A movie director so rich, he'd decided to end the world.

Cut! booms the director. *I've got all I need!*

Pinging in the field. What's pinging in the field? Louder and louder, the pinging.

Oh, it's my phone.

Slowly open my eyes, emerge from my hypnopompic state, roll off the bed and scrounge on the floor for wherever my cell phone went. In my rage, it flew to places unknown. Where is it, under the bed? Everywhere, shards of glass from the broken Mason jar. I cut my hand as I crawl.

Ah, here it is.

It's my sister Mabel blowing up my phone. Twenty texts. *Twenty*? I get it, I ruined the guest room. Offended Terry who I'm sure reached out to her by now. But no, it's vacay pictures.

"Something to cheer you up!"

I open the images.

My nephew pointing at a gorgeous Caribbean sunset. Bright pinks. Yellows. Oranges. Bands across the sky.

The three of them are on a glass-bottomed boat. Water the color of turquoise. To the bottom, crystal clear. Pictures of their feet. My sister's toenails are painted coral. Mark's toes in Adidas slider sandals. And the baby's pudgy feet squeezed in the camera shot.

Sitting around a table at the resort. Coconuts in front of them spouting colorful paper umbrellas. A smaller coconut, sized just for the baby. A rubber nipple on top. These resorts think of everything.

In a conga line. The baby is strapped to Mark's back. Mark is looking back at the baby like baby, are you okay? My sister holds onto Mark's waist and looks at the two of them, her husband, and her son. Her smile is as wide as the world.

I remember when the baby was born, and I'd gone to visit at the hospital, Mark had tears in his eyes. *I've always wanted to be a father.* I hugged him and cried. A tender moment between us I hadn't thought of in a while. In the depths of my depression, all I thought of was the worst.

Depression had a way of doing this: tinting my view in gray.

So many more images. What a beautiful family. Mark. Mabel. The baby. Living their best lives. Doing things together. Out there, doing things.

At the sink in the guest bathroom, I bandage my cut hand. Gauze. Medical tape. First Aid supplies I'd found in the baby's nursery. There we go, that's better.

"Oh Chance, this isn't it, is it?"

Chance looks up at me. He's sitting next to iLitter, purring happily. He sure loves that thing.

"Everywhere I go, my problems follow me. Does that mean *I'm* the problem? Still, it doesn't seem fair. Like what can I do differently to be a better witch? If it's not being broke, and it's not being rich, then what is the answer?"

Chance rubs against my leg.

"Thanks, Chance."

Downstairs in the kitchen, I find things to clean up broken glass. A broom and a dustpan. A paper bag for shards. Looking down I realize I'd gotten blood on my shirt. Yikes. Guess I need to do laundry. Head towards the garage— is that where the washer is? —only to be stopped. The sound of a camera, zooming. A sudden text from Mabel:

"Don't go in the garage."

In the camera, I indicate my shirt. As in, I need to wash it.

"Laundry room is to your left."

I text her a thumbs up.

Throw my shirt in the wash. Get the cleaning tools from the kitchen. Climb the stairs to the bedroom. These floating stairs, I swear.

Never thought I'd miss a railing.

Sweep up broken glass. Scoop up wilted flowers. Sop up the pool of water with a fancy towel. Make the bed again. Tidy up in general. Everything was as it was. As if I'd never raged.

Don't go in the garage.

What did she mean by that?

I need to talk to Ma. I brought my scrying mirror. I take it into the nursery and sit in the rocking chair.

What happened to your hand?

"I cut it on some glass."

Goodness, Fern. You've always been so reckless.

"Really? I thought I was a worrywart."

Well, you're that too. You're both.

I wave my hand in the air.

"Check it out, I'm here at Mabel's. What do you think about that?"

I think it's wonderful. How did it come about?

I give this a thought.

"You know, it's kind of strange but it happened because of Rose. When she died, I mean. It got us talking again."

I look around the room.

"But it's not for me, Ma."

What's not for you?

"This kind of rich person's life. Living in a house like this? This house has got no soul."

You're saying you miss the complex.

"Yes, I suppose I am."

A funny sensation then. Did my mother have a hand in this? I'm about to ask her when she interrupts.

It may not be for you but it's a form of progress. Sometimes we have to do things we don't want to do. That's how we grow. Change.

My scrying mirror goes dark.

I watch more TV. A documentary about Tina Turner. Tina finds true love at age fifty. How does she find it? She finds it when her record company sends a handsome thirty-year-old Swiss man to pick her up at the airport. They fall in love immediately. Interviewed separately, he comes across as gentle and sweet and supportive as she says he is and was from the start. She's eighty now, he's sixty. They're still madly in love. Hours after she's left the room, "Tina stays on my skin like sunlight."

Turns out being a body in a house is harder than I thought.

For one thing, I can't sleep—and not on account of Mabel's texts. It's the food Terry provided. The food is very rich.

Heartburn and indigestion follow me like dogs. I burn through Pepto-Bismol, throwing back shots of pink. Snack on antacids like candy.

My stomach is a mess.

What to do but get up and sit on their big white couch. It takes up the living room. Wraps around like stadium seating. Cup holders. Footrests. The works. Each person has their own seat, but all the seats are attached.

On my lap is Ma's Book of Shadows. Like the scrying mirror, I brought it with me. It's comforting to read. Push a button that opens the shades of their windows. Stare at the pitch-black nothingness. Until a light clicks on and floods their property. What triggered the light, a bug?

But bugs were dead in winter.

I could never live in a place like this, a place divorced from nature. At least at the complex, I could see the stars. Could sit on my porch at night and observe the cosmos. Here, I could not. Floodlights overpowered.

This is interesting. I'm on a page where my mother has drawn an inverted triangle. The triangle is formed by the word 'ABRACADABRA'. At the top of the triangle, the word is fully written. Then as the triangle goes down, one letter is removed. Until at the very bottom, all is left is 'A'.

I wonder what the spell is for.

Chance thumps down the stairs. Meow! Meow! Meow! Escalating to caterwauling, his visceral belly wailing, his primal communication that something is terribly wrong. In the hall I find him pacing. He stops in front of a door.

"Chance, that's the garage. Mabel said it's off-limits."

Chance will not stop crying.

"Okay, we'll do a quick check."

At the motion of my body, the garage illuminates. Harsh. Nearly blinding. I let my eyes adjust. When they do, the first thing I notice is a glaring absence. Ma's jet ski, gone. Sold, as Mabel said. In its place on the floor is a jet-black circle. An upside-down pentagram. A goat's head in the middle.

The seal of the Church of Satan.

I get a closer look. The seal is as large as a basketball court logo. Professionally done. Slick.

Mabel and Mark were Satanists?

The father of my aborted child was a member of the Church of Satan. They espoused individualism at all costs. Prized personal fulfillment. The indulging of every desire. Above all, prioritized the Self.

"What are you doing in the garage?"

Two o'clock in the morning and Mabel's texting me.

"Chance thought he heard something. I wanted to come check."

"I told you not to go down there."

"Yes, I know, but—"

The lights go out. I wave my arms to trigger them. The lights do not turn on. I wave my arms again. The lights do not turn on. Feel my way like a zombie, arms straight in front of me.

I am in the darkest house I have ever known.

I text my sister, "Power's out," but she does not reply. A blackout? A storm? Or was this house possessed? In the grips of a demon?

Only one way to find out.

By the glow of my cell phone, I find the broom in the kitchen—the very same broom I'd used to clean up broken glass. No, it wasn't my broom, but it would have to do. Take it outside. Straddle. Okay, here we go.

Ascend over Mabel's house.

Fly a bit higher to get a view of the neighborhood.

Moonlight directs my way as I loop cul-de-sacs.

A bit higher and a bit higher. Clouds give me welcome hugs. I've missed you too, clouds. But I'm here now, flying. Like riding a bike, isn't it?

House after house electrified. Porch lights, on. Driveways, illuminated. The entire town looks fine. Only Mabel's house was trying to kill me.

But what of Chance? Chance! I'd forgotten about Chance! Slowly descending a staircase, I return to earth. In the house, call for my friend.

A pair of glowing green eyes.

"Chance, is that you?"

A snarling. A rasping.

"You're not Chance, you're a demon! Show yourself to me! Out of the shadows, now!"

The demon shows itself. A pair of horns. Cloven hooves. A stench like rotting vegetables. It hops on the big white couch and does a terrible dance. Whipping its tail. Spitting. My mother's Book of Shadows is open to a page: the inverted triangle of 'ABRACADABRA'.

I grab the tome and squint my eyes and focus all my energy. Focus, Fern, focus. You can banish this demon. You have it in you. You do.

You have got to believe.

I read it as it's written. Remove one letter at a time. From the top to the very bottom. Down to the letter 'A'. It sounds like gibberish.

The demon convulses. Seizes. Constricts to a hairy ball. Smaller and smaller and smaller.

Then it's nothing at all.

Enough watching TV. If I could do anything in the world, what would that thing be? The answer's so easy, it's stunning: I would do my art.

Years had gone by since I'd picked up a pencil. Dipped my brush in watercolors. Messed around with charcoals. Blending stumps. Kneadable erasers. Pastels.

I really missed my tools.

For the time being, I drive to Michaels to pick up supplies. A set of pencils. Markers. A sketch pad to get me started.

Chance reemerges from wherever he hid. Finds a new hiding place in the bag. His green eyes peered out. Large and content.

I'm drawing on the couch. Whatever I think or feel, wherever the pencil goes, I will not judge the result. I'm done being hard on myself. I mean, I banished a demon. What witch can banish a demon? A good witch, that's who.

These markers are pretty cool.

My last job was working at an art gallery in New York City. I commuted from the next town over which had a train station.

On opening night, an impressive-looking man strolled in with an ivory cane. He was wearing a fine Italian suit. Fancy shoes buffed to a shine. Gold rings on all his fingers. He said he was there from Europe to exclusively purchase art. Helped himself to wine and cheese and schmoozed amongst the guests. Left after twenty minutes, winking at me behind the desk.

"Who was that?" I asked Roy, the owner of the gallery.

Roy rolled his eyes. "That guy? He's a homeless artist. Comes here every opening night pretending to be somebody. Years ago, I rejected his portfolio, and he's haunted me ever since."

"Does he always dress like that?"

"No. Last time, he was a woman, as I recall. Full drag, making a scene. Richard showed him out. Caused too much of a ruckus."

Behind the desk, I thought: That man is a magician. A shapeshifter. A Loki. He's being who he wants to be.

And didn't we have the power to harness our identities? For we were not fixed beings; all the time, we changed.

And I held that man in my mind's eye and thought of him as my hero.

"Fern, will you do me a favor and run to get more wine?"

My cell phone lights up: MABEL. Now what? I banished a demon from your house. Wasn't that enough? Except it isn't Mabel.

"It's the baby," says Mark.

"Why? What's wrong? What's going on with the baby? Is my sister okay?"

"Your sister's fine but the baby is running a high fever. It came on suddenly. The doctors here say it could be an allergy. Said we should fly home."

At that moment, I was sketching an image of a rose. The pencil rolled on the floor. I left it there and listened. My sister's voice in the background says something to Mark. He cuts out for a moment, then gets back on the phone.

"Oh Mark, I'm so sorry."

He sniffles.

"We're hoping to get a flight sometime this afternoon. The first one we can get, we're taking it."

More chatter, more like wailing. From a baby or adult, it's hard to tell.

"We're new at this. We'll be seeing you soon."

▼

During the day I pack. Not that I've got much. Turn off iLitter and set it by the front door. A reminder to take it with me. Later that night, the sound of the garage door opening is my cue for crating Chance.

All the lights are on as they enter through the garage. So bright, it's like daytime in here.

The two of them look frazzled. Their minds are somewhere else. Their vacation cut short. Nothing is picture perfect.

"Is there some way I can help?"

Mark brings in their luggage. "No, Fern, that's okay. You've done enough watching the house."

My sister is in the kitchen having passed me with the baby. She's rocking it in its carrier set upon the island. The baby is beet red.

Normally Mabel is put together. Hair done. Makeup. Cute outfit. But Mabel's falling apart. Hair up in a greasy bun. Rings beneath her eyes. Baggy sweatsuit. Puffer coat, unzipped.

I ask her what I asked Mark.

"Is there some way I can help?"

My sister glances up.

"Know any spells for fevers?"

A knowing passes between us.

"Wait right there."

I get our mother's Book of Shadows and place it on the island. Rifle through the pages. Something for fevers, something for fevers. Come on, come on, come on. Ah, here we go.

"Hey Mabel, look at this. I bet Ma used this for us."

My sister scans the spell.

"Fern, I think you're right."

Our mother made notations in the margins of the page. *Worked for M and F. Highly effective.*

"What do we need?"

"A healing circle."

Mark walks into the kitchen.

"Hey, what's going on?"

"Hubs, we need you to cast this spell."

Mark looks at the two of us.

"You're kidding, right?"

"No, we're totally serious."

"All three of us, join hands."

We encircle the baby. Our arms are around the kitchen island, the baby in the center. Like a pupil in the middle of an eye. Sparkling. Healthy. Better.

The baby's fever breaks.

▼

Before I leave, Mark cuts me a check for a thousand dollars. Exactly as promised.

"Mark, it's okay. Forget it. I don't want the money."

Mark scrunches up his face.

"Don't be ridiculous. It's the least we can do. You need the money so take it."

He presses the check in my palm. I look at the amount. A thousand dollars like nothing. I hand him back the check.

"What I want is an apology."

"An apology? For what?"

We're standing in the foyer. Our voices, echo. Wherever my sister is, I know she can hear us.

"When you and Mabel were dating, you called me a cold fish."

"I did?"

"Yes, you did. I was pretty upset."

He rubs the back of his neck.

"Fern, what can I say? I was an idiot. Young and dumb and full of—"

I hold up my hand.

"I like to think I've grown since then."

I pick up Chance's crate.

"Here, let me get the door."

Witches were of the people. Someone you could go to if you were having problems. An accessible, utilitarian person who had boundless expertise, and never made you feel bad about seeking help. Who'd say to you, "I've just the thing!" when you spoke of heartbreak. Handing you a totem with instructions for proper use. Or mixing up a potion addressing physical ailments. Or giving you words to say when your mind was spinning out.

We need witches in our lives, is what I'm trying to say.

The first thing I do when I get home is knock on Nonna's door. The last time I did this was when Rose fell at the quarry. This poor woman. All she has been through. So much loss.

A body moves behind the door. Shuffling. Locks unlocked. Nonna, seeing me, brings a hand to her mouth. Tears well in her eyes.

"Nonna, I'm so sorry."

She wipes away her tears, then motions with her arm. "Call me Maryanne. Please, come in."

Inside her cramped unit, Maryanne offers me a chair. "Can I get you a cup of tea?" She shuffles sideways to her galley kitchen. On TV, Dr. Oz is talking about supplements. Administering a true/false quiz to eager audience members. Calcium pills can cause heart attacks.

I think to myself: true.

Maryanne at the stove boils water in a kettle. Clanks cups in saucers. Tears open tea packets. She asks if I want milk. I tell her I take it plain. Me too, she says. Plain.

Finally, a whistle screams.

"Show's a repeat," Maryanne says, bringing in a tray. "Next he's going to ask if

Vitamin C stops colds."

Dr. Oz asks the audience if Vitamin C stops colds. Shocked faces when he says it doesn't. But Vitamin C is good for you so continue taking it.

Maryanne sits in her recliner.

"Maryanne, look, I—"

"Fern, it's alright. It was a terrible accident. Rose's death was not your fault."

She hands me my tea.

"But I feel awful about it. Could I have gotten to Rose sooner? Was there anything I could have done?" I look down at my cup.

"If you think you feel awful, imagine how I feel. Neighbors are saying things about me."

"Like what?"

"For one, they're calling me a hoarder. Saying where Rose lived was not fit for a child."

"But you gave Rose a home when her mother went away."

"Well, that's the other thing. They say I was neglectful of what happened to my daughter. That her absence was my fault, too."

We go quiet for a while. Sit and drink our tea. Dr. Oz behind a desk gives his closing remarks. Credits roll and all of them belong to

Dr. Oz.

"Rose was a friend to me. She came at a dark time when I needed her."

Maryanne touches my arm. "Same for my granddaughter. When her mother went into the group home, Rose was lost. But you made Rose feel special. She loved playing with you."

I look at a box of toys. Crystal on the top. The wings of Frank and Francine. The zebra mane of Zack. What were the toys in the end?

"How is Rose's mother?"

Maryanne shakes her head. "My daughter is very troubled. I don't know how she'll manage. But she's with people who can help her. What else can I do?"

Will I come to this home again or will this be my last visit? I treat it like it's my last until Maryanne says differently.

"You're welcome here anytime, Fern. Please don't be a stranger."

"Geez, Ma. My place is such a mess. Looking around, it's like—*sheesh*. I've got to clean."

Ma in the scrying mirror is stationed on my altar. Around her burn black candles to clear the energy. Something I should have done before I left for Mabel's. I felt it as soon as I opened the door. It engulfed me like a fog. Old, toxic energy. Not who I was anymore.

You know what to do, Fern.

Everywhere, dust. In the corners, cobwebs. Furballs the size of tumbleweeds drifting across the floor. The smell from the kitchen drain. The stickiness of the linoleum. Not to mention me: I needed a shower. Crawling on my skin like a thousand spider legs.

"I'm feeling overwhelmed."

Do it for your mother, would you?

I clean as best I can to honor my mother's presence. Starting with the altar. Soon I get on a roll and clean my entire unit. As much as I can tackle—I hadn't cleaned in months; the accumulation of dust and filth would need a second tackle—but yes, I clean my unit. Pop in Siouxsie and the Banshees and get down to business.

Two hours later, things are looking nice.
No, not bad at all. This could be a place where
I would like to live.

With Ma's jet ski I would have built a shrine. I've seen such shrines in Mexico. I've seen such shrines in India. I've seen such shrines in Japan. Pictures of them online. Flowers. Fruits. Nuts. Votives. Her jet ski is in the center of it all like a placid Buddha. Raised on a carved stone dais met with sacred bows. Genuflectors on mats sitting, praying, thinking. Communing with Ma's WaveRunner to see what peace it brings.

About the Author

Jessica Bonder is the author of the chapbook, *Bell and Light* and the novella, *Broke Witch*. Her stories have appeared in *The Stockholm Review, The Lonely Crowd, Hotel, Split Lip Magazine, Occulum, BULL, FIVE:2:ONE, STORGY*, and others. She lives in New Jersey. Visit her at www.jessicabonder.com and on Twitter @jessbonder

About the Publisher

Thirty West Publishing House
Handmade Chapbooks (and more) since 2015
www.thirtywestph.com / thirtywestph@gmail.com
You should follow us! Consider being a patron?
Review our books on Amazon & Goodreads
@thirtywestph